M

HOW TO SURVIVE IN THE JUNGLE
BY THE PERSON WHO KNOWS

Lee Aucoin, *Creative Director*
Jamey Acosta, *Senior Editor*
Heidi Fiedler, *Editor*
Produced and designed by
Denise Ryan & Associates
Illustration © Mike Gordon
Rachelle Cracchiolo, *Publisher*

Teacher Created Materials
5301 Oceanus Drive
Huntington Beach, CA 92649-1030
http://www.tcmpub.com
Paperback: ISBN: 978-1-4333-5599-8
Library Binding: ISBN: 978-1-4807-1721-3
© 2014 Teacher Created Materials

WRITTEN BY
BILL CONDON

ILLUSTRATED BY
MIKE GORDON

Contents

DISASTER: I LOVE IT!

Who am I? I'm Bradley D. Mented, that's who. I'm a wild and crazy star, and you're watching my TV show, *The Wild and Crazy Survivor Show!*

What a day I had today! Let me tell you about it. First, my plane ran out of fuel. Sure, I tried to glide. But then, the wings fell off. I jumped out. Halfway down, I realized I'd forgotten my parachute. It was too late to go back for it. Luckily, I had a soft landing. I fell right into the mouth of a hungry hippo!

For a moment, I thought I might be in trouble. But then, just as its jaws were about to snap shut, I remembered! Hippos hate to be kissed. I kissed that hippo as hard as I could. It spat me out and made a face. Then, it sank under the water.

4

Now, here I am, lost and alone in the deepest, darkest jungle.

This is my kind of day!

By the way, when I said I was alone, I forgot to mention the camera operator, the director, and the animal wranglers. And of course, there are medics, catering staff, make-up artists, and bodyguards. Apart from them— and a TV audience of 26 million—I am totally alone!

7

Chapter Two

BEWARE WHAT YOU WEAR!

In the next thrilling episode, I will explain how you, too, can survive in the deepest, darkest jungle. If I can do it, so can you!

The first thing you'll need to do is decide what to wear. I suggest you buy a Swiss Army hat. With the simple push of a button, it can be used as a sleeping bag, a tent, or a life jacket. Some people even use it as a hat!

Wear a very thick shirt in case of tiger bites. Shoes are important, of course. It's best to buy the camouflage ones. That way, the snakes don't see you coming. Finally, only wear shorts that have been coated with anti-lion spray. The lions still might eat you, but they won't enjoy it!

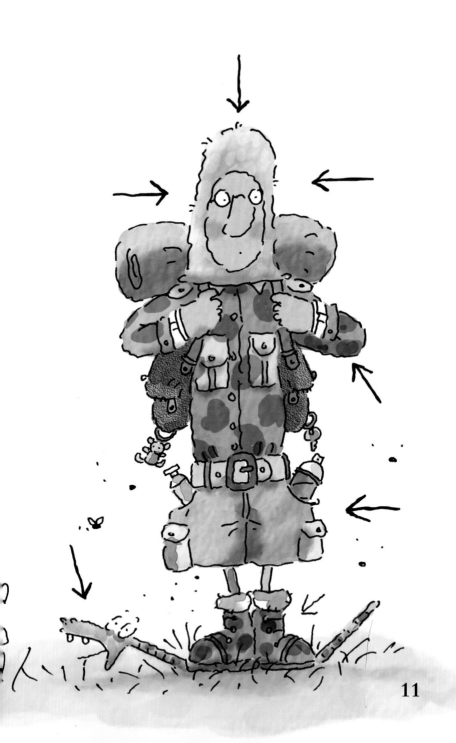

11

Chapter Three

ALWAYS SMILE AT A CROCODILE!

The next thing you must know is how to survive an attack in a fierce jungle. There are two basic skills to learn.

Surprisingly, a lot of people get scared if a crocodile is about to eat them. But crocs can smell fear. It makes them hungry. What you should do is smile. Don't run away. Just lie down, close your eyes, and smile. Three times out of ten, you won't be eaten! Or try standing perfectly still and pretending you're invisible. This only works one in every ten times, but it makes a fantastic TV show!

Chapter Four

FAST FOOD, JUNGLE STYLE!

Now, let's look at what you can eat in the jungle. There's something for everyone!

Contrary to popular belief, you can eat poisonous berries and mushrooms. You can even drink the toxic water. But, believe it or not, there are some people who just won't eat poisonous food. Wimps!

It's true there are a few tiny side effects. For example, your nose hair could grow so long it covers your face. Or you might only be able to see in black and white. And instead of hearing words when people speak to you, you may only hear car alarms. Or you could turn green. But never fear! These symptoms only last for a month or two. So enjoy!

19

Chapter Five

WHEN IN THE JUNGLE, GO APE!

And now, we come to the topic of hygiene in the jungle. Really, there's just one thing to remember.

Forget being clean! It's not possible.
Do you think Tarzan ever had a bath?
Of course not. I can prove it, too.
When he met Jane, he said, "Me
Tarzan." And she said, "You stink!"
Trust me, smelling bad is good. You'll
fit right in with the apes. They might
even make you part of their family. It's
cool living in the jungle! You never
have to brush your teeth or change
your underwear. So forget about
packing all those boring items like
soap and toothbrushes. The only thing
that might come in handy is a large
clothespin for your nose!

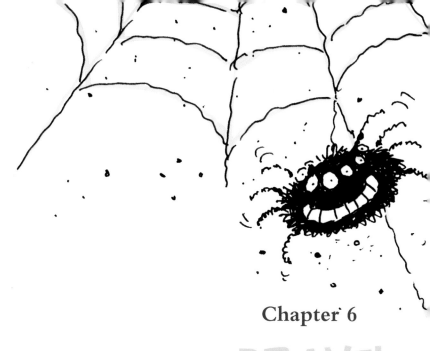

Chapter 6

BEING BRAVE!

Every explorer must be brave. At any moment, you could be stomped into dust by a herd of charging ostriches, or dribbled to death by a flock of swooping dribbler birds.

There are also other little challenges, like giant vines that leap out from nowhere. They can strangle you as you sleep. And watch out for spiders as big as ponies! Don't stumble into their webs. You may never come out!

Through all this, you must whistle a happy tune and hold your head up high. Be brave—just like me! The only thing that scares me is sleeping in the dark without my teddy bear. But that's normal, isn't it?

So there you are, action lovers. This is your complete guide to surviving in the jungle! It will be dangerous. It will be deadly. But it will be so much fun! Can't wait to see you out there.

27

Bill Condon lives in the seaside town of Woonona, Australia. When not writing, Bill plays tennis, snooker, and Scrabble, but hardly ever at the same time. Bill wrote *Pipeline News, Race to the Moon,* and *The Human Calculator* for Read! Explore! Imagine! Fiction Readers.

Mike Gordon was born in England, but he has lived in Santa Barbara, California, for many years. Mike's cartoons have brought him worldwide acclaim, and many of the books he has illustrated are enjoyed in more than eighteen countries. Mike also illustrated *The Zoo and You: A Guidebook* for Read! Explore! Imagine! Fiction Readers.